Also by Colin Dann

Novels
THE ANIMALS OF FARTHING WOOD
IN THE GRIP OF WINTER
FOX'S FEUD
THE FOX CUB BOLD
THE SIEGE OF WHITE DEER PARK
IN THE PATH OF THE STORM
THE BATTLE FOR THE PARK

Picture Books
THE ANIMALS OF FARTHING WOOD
THE FLIGHT FROM FARTHING WOOD

First published in Great Britain 1994 by William Heinemann Ltd
an imprint of Reed Children's Books
Michelin House, 81 Fulham Road, London SW3 6RB
and Auckland, Melbourne, Singapore and Toronto
Reprinted 1994 (twice), 1995 (twice)
The Animals of Farthing Wood copyright © 1979 Colin Dann
Original stories © Colin Dann 1981, 1982, 1983
Adapted by Clare Dannatt
Adaptation copyright © 1994 Reed International Books Limited
Illustrations copyright © 1994 Reed International Books Limited
ISBN 0 434 97501 X
A CIP catalogue record for this book is available at the British Library
Printed and bound in Great Britain by BPC Paulton Books Ltd

The
ANIMALS
of
FARTHING
WOOD

Friends and Enemies

A story by Colin Dann

Illustrated by
Stuart Trotter

HEINEMANN

The Arrival of Winter

The late autumn sun disappeared behind a dark cloud, and a sudden wind sent the last few leaves spinning off the trees. In White Deer Park a tiny creature hopped shivering towards a grassy hollow.

"Toad!" cried an old badger who was sitting in the hollow. "Haven't you hibernated yet? It's getting late!"

"Had to say goodbye to you chaps first!" puffed the toad. "Couldn't forget my old friends from Farthing Wood, could I?"

The toad sat down to wait for other animals to arrive at the hollow. For these were not old inhabitants of the Nature Reserve, but wild creatures who had fled together from their home in Farthing Wood.

They had travelled many miles to find peace in the park. And although they had scattered to build new homes in the trees, in the earth and by the water, they still met together in the hollow from time to time. Somehow, they could not forget the Oath they had made on the journey to protect one another.

"See you in the spring, then," said Toad at last. "Have a good winter!"

"It'll be a hard one," muttered Badger. "I feel it in my bones."

"Yes," added the animals' old leader, Fox. "Tell Adder if you see her to dig down deep. Below frost level."

"Just what I would have said myself," added Tawny Owl from her perch. She liked to be the one to give advice.

Fox watched Toad hopping eagerly towards his winter sleep. "I think Toad and Adder and the hedgehogs are going to be the lucky ones this year," he said, half to himself. "I just hope we're all going to be here to welcome them when they wake up."

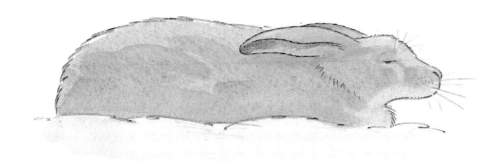

The Oath is Kept

The snow lay crisp and thick on the ground. A hare limped through the trees, blinking at the bright white light.

"Found anything to eat, Hare?" called Owl from a frosty branch. She was shivering despite her ruffled feathers.

"Nothing," sobbed Hare.

"We're all hungry," squeaked the fieldmice. "There isn't one blade of grass left!"

"Fox will help us," said Weasel. "He's so clever, he'll know what to do."

"Fox! Fox!" clamoured the animals. "Our leader will know what to do!"

They gathered excitedly outside Fox's earth, waiting for him to return from his hunting. At long last they spotted him coming back through the trees. But could this be their Fox? Where were his alert look and shining coat, and his powerful run?

Fox crept up to the waiting animals. His ribs stuck out and his fur was scruffy. He gazed at them all with dull eyes. Behind him his beloved Vixen hung her head.

"I can't help you," said Fox, so quietly they could hardly hear him. "We can barely find enough to keep ourselves alive."

Suddenly the anxious animals heard a piercing whistle up above them. Whistler the heron! The bird flew down and landed beside Fox. He flapped his wing with the old bullet hole wound in it extra hard, so that it whistled more than ever. "I've found food!" he croaked. "Lots of crayfish up river where it isn't frozen!"

"Lucky you," said Owl sarcastically.

"But there's enough for everybody," protested Whistler. "And my lovely mate and I can fish them out for you. I remember the Oath you taught me even if you don't," continued Whistler pointedly. "Farthing Wood animals will always help and protect one another. All for one and one for all."

"The Oath! The Oath!" piped the animals. "All for one and one for all."

"Well, now you mention it," said Owl thoughtfully, "I was going to suggest that we birds could hunt a bit further afield and bring back scraps for everyone..."

Fox felt stronger after his meal of crayfish, but he was still worried. He paced his earth restlessly.

"The animals look up to me and I'm failing them," he muttered. "The fieldmice have lost half their families already. They'll never trust me again."

"You can't be expected to stop the snow falling or the wind blowing," Vixen chided her mate gently. "And the birds are doing their best."

Fox smiled a small smile. "You comfort me," he said. "But I must do something. And here comes another friend expecting me to feed him."

Mole, who was hurrying urgently towards Fox, had something other than food on his mind. "It's Badger," sobbed Mole. "I can't find Badger. I've looked everywhere for him, and he's not in his set and he's not in his tunnels and...and..." And poor Mole collapsed in tears at the loss of his special friend.

"There, there. I expect he's just wandered off and will be back soon," soothed Vixen. She glanced at Fox and saw that there was something like the old gleam in his eye. Here was a problem he could do something about.

"We'll send out a search party," barked Fox, a leader once more. "Hare is a fast runner, and Kestrel can keep watch from the sky."

Hare and Fox struggled through the deep snow as best they could. "Badger! Badger!" they called into the eerie winter silence; there was no reply. Kestrel hovered above the park for hours, but she caught no sight of Badger either.

Night fell and the next day came and went, and still there was no Badger. Fox rested wearily in his earth. The gleam had gone from his eye. He had lost more strength and was hungrier than ever. And all for nothing.

Poor Mole could not give up the search. He tunnelled through the hard earth, poking his nose out of the ground every so often to peer blindly about him. He was crying so much that he did not notice a large ginger cat until it was almost on top of him.

"Don't go!" miaowed the cat as Mole backed furiously down his tunnel. "I've got news of Badger!"

Mole stopped in his tracks.

"Badger!" miaowed the cat again. Mole shot back to the surface.

"Your friend Badger broke his leg, but my human friend the Warden found him, and he's at home with me in the Warden's cottage," the cat told Mole. "Badger said to tell you he's fine and will be home soon."

The cat fluffed up his ginger fur and shook the snow off his left paw. "Doesn't seem much like home to me," he added. "I'm going back to my fire and my food." And the cat turned tail and disappeared as quietly as he had come.

Poachers

Badger behaved very strangely when he came back to the park. He was plumper than Mole remembered, and his coat was shiny and sleek. And the only idea he could think of to help the hungry animals from Farthing Wood was that they should all go and live in the Warden's cottage!

"Badger's gone soft in the head," hooted Owl scornfully. "What does he think we are? A bunch of ginger cats?"

"Leave Badger alone," said Vixen. "When we wild creatures have been tamed by humans we need time to adapt back to our usual ways. Badger will be his old self in a few days' time."

Vixen was right.

"Sorry I said some foolish things," mumbled Badger at a meeting in Fox's earth. "Wasn't quite myself, you know..."

"Think nothing of it, old chap," said Owl in a knowing way.

"But I still think humans could help us," continued Badger. "Why don't we go outside the park and hunt for their leftovers?"

"Good idea!" barked Fox, secretly breathing a sigh of relief. Badger was his reliable old friend and helper once more. If he and Badger could learn to raid human dustbins the animals might survive!

And so it was that, although thin and weak, the animals of Farthing Wood no longer felt such dreadful pangs of hunger.

"We knew Fox would save us," they piped, nibbling on the crusts of toast and old bones and potato peelings that had been rescued from the wasteful humans.

"Humans can be quite useful after all," murmured Fox contentedly to Vixen, safely curled up in his earth after another successful raid on nearby houses.

Suddenly, a dreadful bang echoed through the wood.
Fox and Vixen jumped up.

"What was that?" whispered Vixen.

"A shotgun," shuddered Fox.

"Here, in this wildlife sanctuary?" gasped Vixen.

"I must go and see what's happening," said Fox
grimly.

"Be careful," pleaded Vixen, but Fox was already
gone.

Fox ran towards the open parkland where the white
deer roamed. He found the deer running around in a
panic. Even the Great White Stag was pawing the
ground anxiously.

"Poachers!" boomed the Stag. "Our Warden has been taken to hospital. The poachers know we are unprotected."

"They will kill us all and take our valuable skins," cried a doe helplessly.

"Not if I can help it," said Fox. "You welcomed us into your home. Now it's our turn to get you out of trouble."

The Stag looked puzzled and relieved at the same time. "So strange, this concern you animals from Farthing Wood feel for one another, and now for us. Your famous Oath must be something special. Quite unlike the law of the wild! But what can you do to stop these poachers?"

"I must think," said Fox, slightly embarrassed by the Stag's praise.

Vixen did not like the plan Fox came up with. "You're putting your life in danger — perhaps for nothing," she protested.

But Fox was firm. That night when the poachers returned, he was ready for them. Crouching low in the shadows, Fox watched the herd of white deer huddling together, ghostly in the moonlight. Then he heard the crunch of human footsteps in snow and the snapping of twigs as dark shapes crept through the trees towards their goal. Fox waited, his heart pounding.

Then, "Run!" he barked to the deer.

And as the herd galloped and scattered, Fox streaked out and under the men's feet.

"That fox has disturbed the deer," cried a gruff voice. "Get him!"

But Fox was too quick for them. The men ran after him, stumbling and shooting wildly at anything. At last the poachers gave up, exhausted, and crept out of the park.

One poor doe lay killed by a poacher's shot, but the rest of the herd was unhurt. "You have saved us," said the Stag. "We will never forget your bravery."

"That's the last we'll see of them," said a tired but satisfied Fox. His wise Vixen was not so sure.

The next night, another shot echoed through the woods. Fox ran in the direction of the sound and found a strange fox dead in his path. He froze in horror.

The poachers were seeking revenge on the animal who had thwarted them. They would shoot every fox in the park until they were sure they had got their enemy.

Now it was the Stag's turn to comfort Fox. "We shall help you," he decided. "This Oath has strange powers!"

That night, Owl kept watch. She hooted three times when she saw the men again, and Fox dashed out of hiding into full view of the poachers. But as they ran out to shoot at Fox, the entire herd of deer thundered towards them!

"Help! Help!" cried the poachers. "A stampede!" And they turned and fled.

The frozen pond lay directly in their path. The men rushed onto it to escape from the deer and then there was an awful cracking and splashing sound mixed up with human shouts for help. The poachers had fallen through the ice! It was melting!

The animals of Farthing Wood watched from the trees and bushes as the soaked, shivering men dragged themselves from the pond. It was not deep, just wet and cold.

"Hooray!" cheered the animals when the park was empty of intruders once more. "The poachers are beaten. And the ice is melting! It's spring at last!"

Spring Returns

A light breeze stirred the trees in White Deer Park. Toad felt the spring sun warm his back as he hopped lazily towards the hollow. "Hello, Badger," he yawned.

"Ah, you're awake at last," Badger greeted him. "Nice sleep?"

"Mmm!" said Toad. "Have a good winter?"

Badger shuddered. "You were best off out of it. We didn't all pull through."

Toad's smile vanished. "Who—who's left?" he asked anxiously.

"Fox made it, and so did Kestrel and Owl and Whistler and..." Toad's face brightened again, "and everyone's having babies. Well, almost everyone," said Badger, a little sadly. "Apart from us old bachelors."

"We're not old yet," chipped in Mole, popping out of a hole by Badger's tail. "And now that everyone's awake again we're going to have a party," he added excitedly.

And so it was that one fine spring afternoon, all the animals of Farthing Wood who had made a little corner of White Deer Park their home and survived the terrible winter, flocked towards the hollow.

There they told stories about the old days and shared the food that was now easy to find again.

Fox looked on the assembled crowd with pride. They had all helped one another, and Fox knew in his heart that he had proved himself as the animals' leader. The winter was now a bad dream — a story to tell their children.

The very next day, Fox and Vixen's own first cubs were born.

The Death of Dreamer

Vixen watched tenderly as her four tiny cubs played around her. Their legs were still wobbly, but one, the larger of the two boy cubs, was determined to explore.

"We've called him Bold," Vixen laughed to Badger, who was watching the cubs like a fond uncle.

"And this must be Friendly," said Badger as another boy cub nuzzled at his foot.

"And Charmer," added Fox, smiling proudly at one pretty little daughter.

"But where has that Dreamer got to?" said Vixen. "She's in a world of her own."

Soon Dreamer wandered back to the earth. Vixen cuffed her lightly. "Stay by my side," she said.

Dreamer nodded, but she was thinking about catching butterflies.

Danger was nearer than even Vixen knew. Watching the happy little family was a strange fox, and he was not so happy.

"Those Farthing Wood animals will take over the park," he snarled to his wife later that day. "I've seen their cubs. This park belongs to me. No one gets in the way of Scarface and his tribe."

"They haven't done anything yet, apart from have babies," suggested his mate nervously. "And we have some lovely cubs, too."

Scarface spat. "If it wasn't for them there would have been more food in the park last winter. And if that stupid fox hadn't made the poachers angry they wouldn't have come back and killed some of our tribe." Scarface had seen and heard everything that the Farthing Wood animals had done that winter. "Oath indeed," he continued. "Let's see what happens to their precious Oath when I show them who is king of the park!"

Early that evening, a terrible cry shattered the peace of the park. Vixen came tearing back to her earth, three cubs bounding after her.

"Dreamer!" she screamed. "My little Dreamer is dead!"

Fox dropped a tear onto Dreamer's limp body lying on the ground. Then he looked up angrily.

"Someone who hates us has done this," he snarled. "And whoever he is, he shall pay for it."

"It's that strange fox we saw lurking about yesterday," piped up Weasel.

"I said he was up to no good," added Owl.

Then there was another cry from Vixen. "Bold has vanished! My cubs, my cubs!"

Kestrel swooped down. "I've seen Bold," she called. "That fox they call Scarface has captured him!"

31

None of the animals had noticed little Bold slipping away. They were all thinking about Dreamer.

"I shall get that old fox for killing my sister," Bold thought to himself. "Dad will be really pleased with me!"

Yet when Bold looked up and saw a huge ugly fox with a great long scar, baring its teeth at him, his little heart missed a beat and his little legs trembled. But he was not called Bold for nothing. He bared his teeth back, though they were chattering with fear. Then he ran for it.

Bold was caught easily enough and taken back to Scarface's den. Even then Bold did not give up. When his guard turned his back, Bold escaped. But little did he know as he ran back eagerly towards his parents' earth that his father was on his way towards Scarface's territory to rescue him.

When Bold reached home, expecting to see the welcoming faces of his family and friends, he was greeted instead by angry looks.

"What — what's the matter?" gulped Bold. "Where's my dad?"

"Your father went to look for you," Badger told him sternly. "Friendly went too, and was caught by Scarface. So your father made Scarface let Friendly go — "

"Oh, good," interrupted Bold.

"But Scarface would only let Friendly go if Fox swapped places with him. So now our leader is a hostage, thanks to you."

Bold had never seen Badger angry before. He hung his head in shame.

"We'll do all we can to help," said Badger, a little more kindly. "We're all going up there now."

"If my dad can't escape from Scarface, how will old Badger help?" thought Bold to himself.

Perhaps Badger could have done something, but he did not have to. When the animals from Farthing Wood arrived at Scarface's clearing, they were amazed to see a huge crowd gathered. On one side sat Scarface and his tribe. On the other sat Fox. And in the middle stood the Great White Stag. "The animals of Farthing Wood were welcomed here by us all," declared the Stag. "And they must be allowed to live in peace. They keep to their own land in the park and you, Scarface, shall keep to yours."

The animals scampered back happily to their homes, with Fox in their midst.

"I wonder who could have told the Stag there was trouble?" said Mole.

"I wonder," hissed Adder, slipping away into the bushes silently. The noisy crowd of animals never noticed she was there.

Scarface bit his lip as Fox walked free. "This is my land," he thought to himself. "And it's been the land of my family for generations. We were here before any white deer or park. I'll show them who I am!"

One morning Hare came dashing into the hollow. "My wife," he screamed. "She has been taken by Scarface!" He collapsed on the ground, weeping pitifully. "We survived that journey and got through that awful winter, just for this!" he sobbed.

Fox growled softly in his throat. If Scarface did not respect the authority of the Stag, Fox would have to fight back.

Scarface Attacks

The animals gathered nervously in the hollow. Fox had called a Council of War. He opened his mouth to speak, but at that very moment, Kestrel swooped down out of the sky.

"Disaster! Disaster!" she called. "Adder's killed a fox! But it was the wrong one! Scarface is still alive and he's on the warpath! He's vowed to kill us all."

"Scarface is coming! He'll kill us! He'll kill us!" panicked the rabbits, falling over themselves in their haste to run back to their burrows.

"STOP!" barked Fox. "We'll be safer together. Get into Badger's set—now!"

Their Council of War abandoned, the animals of Farthing Wood fled to the safety of Badger's underground home.

"How many exits has your set got?" Fox asked Badger when the last fieldmouse had scuttled down the tunnel.

"Four," wailed Badger. "We'll never be able to guard them all. And if we block them up we'll be trapped."

"Let's wait and see," said Fox grimly. "Quiet, everybody!"

The animals needed no second warning. You could have heard a feather drop.

The deathly hush was soon broken by the horrible sound of a pack of foxes approaching. The ground above the animals' heads shook and so did the poor rabbits as Scarface's tribe thundered above.

They heard a rasping breath at the main entrance to

the set. "I know you're all in there," Scarface's voice snarled. "And there's no escape. You're surrounded."

The animals knew that this was true. They would all die now.

Then Fox leapt to his feet and walked calmly to the entrance. "I challenge you, Scarface, to single combat," he called. "If you win, all this is your undisputed territory. But if I win, you will not trouble us again."

Scarface was silent for a moment. His honour was at stake. Then: "I accept," he growled.

The animals breathed a sigh of relief. Of course Fox would win. But Vixen shivered anxiously, and gathered her cubs around her.

Fox strode into the clearing in front of Badger's set. Slowly, timidly, the other animals crept out of the set. Their loyalty to Fox overcame their fear, though they shrank back at the sight of Scarface. There was complete silence as the two foxes paced around each other. Who would make the first move?

Without warning, Scarface pounced. He knocked Fox to the ground. The Farthing Wood animals gasped in dismay. Quick as lightning, Fox was back on his feet. He snapped at Scarface, but the bigger animal twisted out of the way before running at Fox and throwing him to the ground again. Fox lay, breathing heavily. He dragged himself onto his feet, panting.

"Farthing Wood, Farthing Wood," chanted the animals uncertainly.

Out of the corner of his eye, Fox saw Vixen and his cubs. His eyes blazed, and this time when Scarface lunged at him, he leapt sideways and Scarface sprawled in the dust. Fox flew onto Scarface's back, and sank his teeth into his neck. "Kill him! Kill him!" shrieked the animals.

Then Kestrel's cry cut through the noise. "The Warden's coming!"

Fox knew it was now or never; in a moment the Warden would separate them. He must kill Scarface. Fox sank his teeth deeper. Then suddenly, unexpectedly, he released his grip and walked away from Scarface. As the Warden approached, the animals scattered and Scarface crawled to safety.

The animals looked at Fox, puzzled. He had saved their lives, but why hadn't he killed Scarface?

"I haven't the killer instinct any more," was all Fox could say.

"Three cheers for Fox," cried Mole. But the cheers were quiet ones. Had Fox really saved them? Would Scarface be back?

The Enemy Defeated

Scarface did plan to come back, but the animals need not have worried. Unlike Fox, Adder's killer instinct was as healthy as it had ever been. While Adder's friends kept close to their homes and did not let their babies out of their sight, she lay low and plotted her revenge on Scarface. She had had an argument with the enemy fox, and rather a short tail to prove it. Adder ate little to save her venom and watched and waited. At last she saw her chance. As Scarface crossed the stream one night, the snake drifted towards him on the current.

Scarface cried out as he felt the pain of Adder's bite. He knew then that he had lost his battle. As he struggled out on the far bank, waiting for the poison to work, Scarface saw Adder's eyes glittering as she floated in the water.

"Farewell, Scarface," she hissed, before drifting on her way.

The news spread like wildfire through the park.

"Scarface is dead! Scarface is dead!" whooped Weasel gleefully.

"We're free!" cried the rabbits.

"Three cheers for Fox!" yelled Mole, as usual.

"I see I'm forgotten once more," hissed Adder to herself. She was too pleased with herself to mind, this time.

Fox had not forgotten Adder, though. He had defeated Scarface in battle, but he knew that it was the snake who had made their lives really safe. Although Scarface had been his mortal enemy, Fox could not bring himself to celebrate the loss of a life. He would concentrate on the future.

"We have lived in our own corner of the park for long enough," he declared.

"Well, why not mingle with the natives, like me?" said Whistler, smiling at Speedy, his mate.

"You're not the only one," said Mole shyly. "Meet Mateless — er, well, that is to say she was mateless, till she found me!" And there by Mole's side was a female mole.

"And this is Paddock!" croaked Toad, hopping up joyfully with a large female toad behind him.

"Well, it seems everyone's been making friends," said Vixen, smiling at Charmer, who giggled. For a long time she had been meeting Scarface's son Ranger secretly. When Fox had first found out, he was furious. Ranger might have been a spy!

But, true to Charmer and his word, Ranger had done nothing to help his father. He had remained neutral in the war between Scarface and Fox. And now he and Charmer could be happy together.

"Let's hope we can live peacefully here for ever," Charmer said to Ranger as they wandered alone together by the stream that evening.

"And Friendly and Bold can make friends with my cousins and sisters," laughed Ranger.

"And our cubs will never know that our fathers were deadly enemies," added Charmer quietly.

Bold, however, was not interested in meeting Ranger's relatives. He felt restless in the park. The battle with Scarface was over and he had taken no real part in it. Bold wanted his own adventures. He wanted to explore the world.

In the Real World

Bold stepped out eagerly through the hole in the fence of the park. He sniffed the crisp night air joyfully. He smelt freedom! Now he would be a bold young fox in his own right, and not just the son of the Farthing Fox. He was in the real world. He could be a true wild creature at last!

Bold ran on until he found a small wood, which he bounded into noisily. He was getting tired, so he was pleased to find an empty badger's set. He crawled into it and fell into a deep and happy sleep.

Bold was woken in the morning by the sound of a badger snuffling around the entrance to her home.

"Thanks for lending me a bed for the night," said Bold cheekily.

The badger looked at him suspiciously. He obviously meant no harm, so she decided to give him some advice.

"No fox stays around in this wood," she said. "The gamekeeper sees to that."

"My name is Bold," laughed the young fox, privately wondering what a gamekeeper was. "Humans hold no fear for me."

Bold spent several days catching the plump and juicy pheasants which he learned the humans kept in the wood. He thought it was good fun to leave the birds' feathers scattered around where he knew the gamekeeper walked. He would never be caught!

One night as Bold trotted through the wood in search of his supper, he heard a dreadful cry of pain that made the hairs on his neck stand up.

Running towards the source of the cry, he found the badger caught in a terrible trap. Bold knew that the trap had been laid for him.

"I'll get you out of this," he muttered, biting at the vicious wire with his strong teeth.

For the first time in his life, the cunning of humans proved almost too much for Bold. Hour after hour he worked, and then he heard the slow heavy tramp of the gamekeeper's footsteps. After a last desperate tug at the wire it snapped and flung itself back into Bold's eye. As the gamekeeper's steps grew nearer, the poor badger struggled free from the trap and hobbled to her set, followed by Bold with blood streaming from his wounded eye.

"Why did you save me?" gasped the badger.

"Because that trap was laid for me," replied Bold grimly.

"Well," said the badger, baffled by the fox's talk as much as by his action, "if you ever need help I shall do the same for you."

"Thank you," said Bold. "But I'll be off now. You were right about this wood."

Bold's sight was blurred now in his injured eye. When he pounced on a vole running foolishly across his path, he missed it and it scuttled away. But he still felt glad to be Bold, roaming the open countryside by night and sleeping in a gorse thicket by day.

One morning he had just dozed off when he was woken suddenly by the sharp crack of gunfire. Peering out from his shelter, Bold saw a line of men aiming their guns at birds flying in panic above them. A pheasant fell with a thud right in front of Bold, and a large dog ran towards him to collect it. In a minute the dog would discover the fox and his life would be over! Bold made a dash for it but he never reached safety. He heard a human shout, "Fox!", another gunshot was fired, and he felt a fierce pain in his right leg.

Bold fell to the ground. The man called off his dog and went back to shooting birds. Bold crawled weakly into a ditch. Now he understood the terrible power of humans.

Son of the Farthing Fox

"**W**ell, well, well! Can you be that same bold young fox I saw a few weeks ago?" croaked an unfamiliar voice in Bold's ear as he lay in his ditch.

Bold looked up wearily to see a giant black crow looking at him with his beady eyes.

"I've been watching you," the crow went on. "And I'm not surprised to see you like this, the way you've been carrying on. Making fun of the humans and prancing about in daylight for all to see."

"Please," groaned Bold. "I've learned my lesson. Can you — would you — perhaps you wouldn't mind — helping me?" Asking for help felt like the hardest thing Bold had ever done.

"Help!" croaked the crow. "Why should I help you?" He flapped his wings impatiently.

Bold knew that in a moment his one chance of survival would slip away. "Because I am the son of the Farthing Wood Fox," he muttered, swallowing his pride.

"What?" shrieked the crow, hopping nearer. "The famous fox who led the animals to White Deer Park? Now I see why you've got all these funny notions about animals helping one another."

The crow jigged from one foot to the other. Then he made his mind up. "Well," he said. "It would never do for me to cause the death of a son of the Farthing Fox. What do you want me to do?"

"There's a badger in the gamekeeper's wood whom I helped once," said Bold quickly, before the crow could change his mind. "Tell her I'm injured and need food." Bold sank back, exhausted by the effort of talking. He knew he had a long wait ahead.

Bold had fallen into an uneasy sleep when he was woken by a familiar snuffling sound. He jerked awake, wincing at the pain in his leg, and blinked. Ambling towards him was not one badger but four! His faithful friend had brought her cubs, and each one held a tasty morsel of food for Bold in its jaws.

Bold drooled at the sight of the food, but tried to be polite. "Thank you for coming all this way for me—" he began.

"Eat up," the badger interrupted. "We've got to get your strength back."

Day by day the badger, whom Bold called Shadow, braved the open fields to bring him food. As he grew stronger he grew more uneasy at the danger she was putting herself into for him. How Bold hated having to rely on others for survival. This was not what he had left White Deer Park for.

Bold felt less anxious about the crow, who ran fewer risks to bring him titbits and was still rude to him. It was easier to cope with the crow's nasty remarks than Shadow's kindness.

"Still idle, then?" cawed the crow one afternoon, spying Bold dozing in his ditch.

"Not for longer than I can help," retorted Bold. "I can trot quite fast now on three legs. And I'll get my own back on these humans."

"Caw! Caw!" laughed the crow. "You'd better come to town with me, then."

"Town?" asked Bold curiously. "What's that?"

"It's where humans live, of course," replied the crow. "You foxes can make a grand living stealing scraps at night."

Bold's good eye lit up. Here was his chance to show those humans, and get enough to eat as well. He knew that he did not have the speed or sharp vision needed to catch live prey ever again.

"Will you lead me there?" Bold asked the crow. "Town sounds like the place for me!"

To the Town

Bold found travelling harder than he let on to the crow. He limped determinedly over fields and through woods for three long nights, resting by day where he could.

On the second evening he looked up and saw a strange orange glow behind the next hill. "Those are the lights of the town," the crow informed him. "There are so many, they light up the sky."

Bold felt his heart beat a little faster, and the hill seemed easier to climb than he had thought it would.

On the third day Bold was woken by a dreadful dull noise ringing in his ears. He shook his head. "Not something wrong with my hearing now, I hope," he muttered.

The crow laughed. "That's the noise of the town you're hearing. It never stops. But it's quieter at night," he added, seeing Bold's unhappy face. "You'll get used to it. Here, I've got you a titbit." And the crow dropped an odd-looking white thing at Bold's feet.

"What's that?" sniffed Bold.

"Don't eat it if you don't want," said the crow. "After all the trouble I took to bring it to you."

Bold chewed a corner and then snapped the rest of it up in one bite. It had meat inside!

"There's plenty more where that came from," said the crow.

"I think I'm getting used to the noise already," replied Bold. "And for stealing me such nice titbits I shall call you Robber! Lead on, Robber."

Bold had never seen so many cars or humans before. He hid on the outskirts of the town, and was grateful to Robber for bringing him food.

By the next evening, despite his injuries and tiredness from the journey, Bold felt something like his old spirit of adventure creeping back. Tonight, he would explore.

"You've been feeding me—now I'll feed you," he announced grandly to Robber. He slipped noiselessly towards the centre of the town.

Bold padded down a narrow alley behind some gardens. He nosed the lid off one of the dustbins Robber had told him about. It was full of the most delicious scraps. Bold ate fast, his nose in the bin, until it tipped over with a clatter. Startled, Bold limped away as fast as he could.

Bold paused, sniffing the air. He wrinkled up his nose, catching an old familiar scent from long ago. The smell of fox! Wary now that he knew he had a rival, Bold slunk forward on his belly. Then he saw the strange fox trotting ahead. A beautiful, swift, lively fox such as he had once been.

Except that this fox was a female. She crouched down and leapt over a fence into a nearby garden.

Bold gazed up at the fence bitterly. He would never clear it. Pressing his nose to the garden gate, Bold watched the female as she jumped daintily up onto a bird table and nibbled at the scraps there. More than anything, Bold wanted to be in that garden with that vixen. He began to dig wildly under the gate, but had only made a shallow hole when he heard a soft thud beside him. He looked up to see the vixen, staring at him.

"That's an odd way to go about it," she said in a low voice. "There's nothing in there, anyway."

61

"No, no," stammered Bold, wondering why his mother had decided to call him that name. "I just thought — well, um, you were there."

The vixen gave him a curious look. "Be seeing you, I expect," she said, and vanished as silently as she had come.

Bold limped back to the outskirts of town, his tail and ears drooping.

"Where's my titbit, then?" asked Robber.

"I don't know," snapped Bold irritably. "I must have dropped it."

In fact he had forgotten all about his promise to Robber.

"Temper, temper," said Robber. "I won't be bringing you anything tomorrow, then. Fair's fair."

"I don't care," muttered Bold. "Town's horrible."

Robber cocked his head on one side. "I expect you'll feel better when you meet another fox," he suggested. "It's not natural for you, keeping company with an old crow like me."

"But I've met a fox, and I feel worse!" howled Bold.

Crow blinked. "Female, was she?"

"How did you know?"

"Oh, just a feeling. Didn't she like you, then?"

Bold's tail wagged slightly. "Well, she did say 'Be seeing you, I expect.' Do you think that means she liked me?"

"I'd give town another go tomorrow, if I were you," advised Robber. "And if you don't come back, I'll understand."

"Well, if you're sure," said Bold. "But if either of us gets into trouble, we can leave a titbit here by this wall. That will be our message to come and look for each other."

That night Bold went back towards the town gardens. His heart skipped a beat when he saw the female fox running towards him. She stopped when she saw him.

"It's you again," she said. Then she added, a little shyly, "Would you like to come hunting with me?"

"I would," said Bold sadly, "but I can't."

"Oh well, in that case..." said the vixen, turning to go.

"No! Don't leave yet," cried Bold. "It's not that I don't want to, it's—it's—my leg, and my eye."

Bold told the vixen how he had been injured.

"You poor thing," she said. "I tell you what—we'll work as a team. I know a canal near here where there's a colony of rats. I can hunt them out and you can stop them getting away."

Bold's mouth watered. He agreed happily.

Early that morning, after the most wonderful night's hunting of his life, Bold let his new friend make room for him in her earth behind a churchyard wall. "I'll call you Whisper," he murmured, before falling fast asleep.

Late summer sunshine turned to autumn winds. The weather got colder, but Bold was plumper now, and his coat was shiny. He and Whisper made a good hunting pair and kept each other company. One winter evening, as they dozed together in their earth, Whisper tried to get Bold to tell her something of his past. She had heard nothing except how Bold was injured.

"I wish you'd tell me some more of your adventures," she coaxed. "You must have had lots — an old fox like you!"

Whisper had meant it as a compliment, but the startled look on Bold's face told her she had made a mistake.

"Old! Me!" cried Bold. "This spring will be my first season. I'm younger than you!"

"Well, I meant kind of seasoned," blustered Whisper. But it was too late.

The next evening, Bold hobbled back to the canal and gazed at his reflection in the water. It was true, he looked old. Why did Whisper want to be with him? Was it just pity? He might as well tell her where he came from. What did it matter, now?

"I was born in White Deer Park, but my family

doesn't come from there," said Bold that evening. "My father led a group of animals from the old Farthing Wood to — "

"The Farthing Fox!" interrupted Whisper, awestruck.

"Yes, that's what they call him," said Bold gloomily.

Whisper jumped up. "Oh, Bold!" she exclaimed. "I knew there was something special about you!"

A keen look came into her eye. But poor Bold was miserable. He had come all this way and he was still in his father's shadow.

A few weeks later, Whisper told Bold that she was expecting cubs. Bold cheered up. Being in town with Whisper was a good life. Now they would have a family...

Whisper broke in on Bold's happy thoughts.

"So," she was saying, "of course we must set out for the park as soon as we can."

"Park? What park?"

"White Deer Park, of course. Our cubs will have the blood of the Farthing Fox. They must be born in the nature reserve."

Bold groaned, and sank down on his front paws. "You only love me for my father," he cried bitterly. "I vowed never to go back to the park."

"Oh, but we must," insisted Whisper. She was so excited that she did not notice how sad and tired poor Bold was.

"Very well," said Bold wearily. "For the sake of the cubs."

At long last, Whisper smelt spring in the wind. She was so eager to be going that Bold had not the heart to delay her any more. But he knew that winter was not over yet, and that the journey would be a hard one.

Without telling Whisper what he was doing, Bold went to the wall on the outskirts of town where he had said goodbye to Robber such a long time ago. He left a scrap of food for Robber, hoping that the bird still went to look there from time to time.

The very next day Bold heard a loud flapping of wings and cawing — and there was Robber.

"I just wanted to tell you that we're leaving," said Bold. "Going back to White Deer Park."

"But I thought you liked town," said Robber.

"I do. But Whisper's going to have cubs, and she wants them there."

Robber saw that Bold would not welcome any questions. "Well," he cawed, "I won't say goodbye. I'll fly along with you, for old times' sake."

One early spring evening, Whisper and Bold set out on the long journey back to White Deer Park. Ahead of them flew the dark shape of Robber.

White Deer Park Again

The travellers had not gone far before Whisper realised how selfish she was being. Bold limped along painfully. But it was too late now to turn back, and Whisper did want Bold to come with her.

A sudden late fall of snow halted their progress in open country. Bold was exhausted by his struggle through the wet snow. He sank down where he stood.

"Bold," urged Whisper. "You can't stop there, in the open!"

"I can't move," he panted. "You go on and find cover, and I'll join you when I'm rested."

Whisper looked at Bold, and started to sob. "You are so brave, and you've come all this way for me, and it's my fault, and —"

"Go," repeated Bold. "For the sake of the cubs."

Those words were the only ones that could have moved Whisper on. All that day she waited in a nearby wood, while Bold lay in the snow. He would die! But Whisper had forgotten that Bold had friends. Robber watched over the wounded fox. He brought him any scraps of food he could find, and even beat off a dog, by diving at the startled animal from the air.

So when Whisper came back that evening, expecting the worst, she was delighted to find Bold sitting up and flexing his stiff legs. She licked his nose excitedly, and they set off once more.

Unknown to Whisper, Bold's strength was draining with every step he took. The nearer they got to White Deer Park, the weaker he felt. One night, when the old familiar smells of the park wafted to him on the breeze, he made a vow quietly to himself.

The next night, they reached the park boundaries.

"I'll rest here now," said Bold to Whisper. "And you can hunt for me before going into the park," he added vaguely. "Goodbye."

"Goodbye for now," said Whisper. She would have loved to run straight into the park. Surely there would be plenty to hunt inside the gates? But she looked at Bold's skinny body and sunken eyes. How could she refuse him?

As soon as Whisper had disappeared, Bold moved from his hiding place. He limped rapidly away from it, searching for another. At last he found a hole in an old tree root. He dug himself in so deep that no one would ever notice him. Apart from Robber.

"What are you up to now?" he cawed.

He tried to sound like his usual cheeky self, to cover up how sad he was feeling. Robber knew that Bold was very ill.

"Don't tell Whisper where I am," said Bold fiercely. "I don't want to die in that park! I shall die as I lived — free and Bold."

When Whisper came running back eagerly with a freshly caught mouse, Bold was gone. Whisper let out a cry and dropped the mouse. "Bold! Bold? Where are you? Come back!"

Whisper searched and searched, but she could not find her mate. In her heart she knew she never would.

"Go into the park, my dear," said Robber gently from a tree. "For the sake of the cubs."

Whisper turned tail and walked quietly into White Deer Park, alone. She had not gone far before she saw a young vixen, also about to give birth to cubs.

"Who are you?" challenged the vixen. She spoke just like Bold did!

"I'm Whisper... I've come a long way, and... Are you Bold's sister?"

"What's that to you?" asked the vixen, who was Charmer.

"He's my mate," blurted out Whisper.

"Your mate!" cried Charmer. "Where is he? Is he here?"

"He's just outside the park, but I can't find him, and I think — I think he's dying," sobbed Whisper.

Charmer ran as fast as she could to her parents' earth. When Fox and Vixen heard her story, they hurried to the edge of the park with Friendly and Charmer. But Whisper stayed where she was, resting in Charmer's earth. She had said goodbye to Bold.

"Bold! Bold! My son!" cried Vixen and Fox, running up and down the paths outside the park. "Where are you?"

Robber watched them from his tree. Bold had told him not to tell anyone where he was. But if Bold died without seeing his parents and brother and sister, Robber would be responsible.

His mind made up, Robber flew down to the little party of foxes. "If you're looking for Bold," he announced, "follow me!"

Vixen scrabbled at the moss and leaves covering Bold's hiding place. "Oh, Bold!" she sobbed. "Is that you?"

Bold stirred. "Mother!"

"Son!" cried Fox. "My brave cub, my Bold."

Bold opened his eyes to see his mother and father, and Friendly and Charmer standing quietly behind them.

"I'm so proud of you," murmured Fox.

"Whisper is safe," said Charmer.

"And all your cubs will hear about your adventures," added Friendly.

Bold said nothing; but he smiled a little smile as he closed his eyes for the last time.

The next day, Whisper gave birth to four healthy cubs. She licked them fondly and counted them carefully. The biggest one wriggled and squirmed. A few weeks later he was the first to stand on his shaky legs.

"You look a bold one to me," laughed Whisper, watching her cubs play. "Now come here and I'll tell you a story."